Samuel T. Moore of Corte Magore

Tonia Allen Gould

~ Art Direction: "Mr. Lawrence" ~
Illustrated by: Marc Ceccarelli and Michelle Fandrey

Samuel T. Moore of Corte Magore

© 2013 Tonia Allen Gould

ISBN-13: 978-1-61813-121-8

Printed in the United States by
Mira Digital Publishing
Chesterfield, Missouri 63005

Dedicated to Whitney:

Once upon a time, there was a spirited little toddler who babbled
the nonsensical words "Corte Magore" from her car seat, playing with
her bare toes while on a drive along the California Coast. Those words
inspired a place that will live forever in my heart. You inspired me then
and you continue to inspire me now. This is for you, kid.

And, to Miles:

You rival me in creativity, and I know you will put that to good use
when you grow up. Always remember the conversation we had
in the car about dreaming. You said, "Hey mom, what if your book
doesn't sell?" I pulled over the car, turned off the ignition, looked you
straight in the eyes and told you that it's okay to dream, and it's
definitely not okay if you don't.

P.S. If you are reading this, my book sold.

None have told this tale before
Of poor, old, Samuel T. Moore
A fiddler crab that clawed his way onto the shore
Of a sandy, white beach called Corte Magore

When Samuel took a beady-eyed look around
He knew he had finally, finally found
A place where he could spend his days
Beneath the sun and ocean's haze

"Here's where I want to settle down!"
He said, as he staked his bow into the ground
"Oh yes, this is where I want to be!"
The old crab said, with crabby glee

But Sam needed shelter at long last
Before the tides came in strong and fast
Before the tides would carry him away
Back out to sea, and north of the bay

His friends, the hermits, all had their own huts
(Made from cracked-open, half-shells of the coconut)
A coconut shell is fine, this is true
But for a fiddler crab, it just wouldn't do

Sam needed someplace of his own to belong
A place to burrow and fiddle, all day long
A home that would stand perfect, strong and true
When the tides rolled in, or the wind simply blew

Yes, Sam would be ready and waiting at the least
Because he was a fighter and the SEA was his BEAST!

So, he set out to work
There was work to get done
He had to be finished by quarter-to-one
By quarter-to-one, the tides would roll in
And Sam, the crab, wasn't in the mood to swim

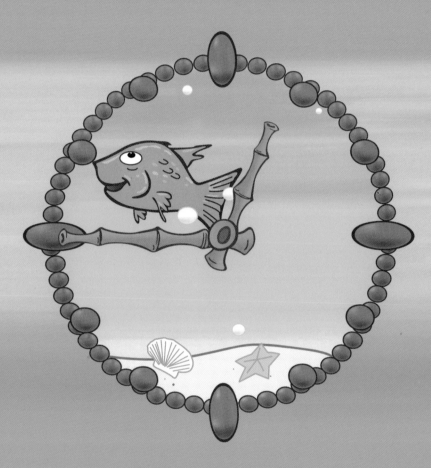

So, he built a new home of driftwood and stick
(Not like my house, or yours, of mortar and brick)
The sticks, he tied them, in tee-pee fashion
Sam thought his new home was a mansion!

The holes were patched with seaweed and kelp
He built it himself, never asking for help
The sand was his yard, and there was lots of it
He imagined he'd stay there…
And play there…
Or just fiddle and sit!

Just as he finished building his new home
His claws were wet and dripping with foam
When the first of the waves rolled up to his door
Poor Sam had to use his fiddle as an oar!

He had to move quickly; there was no time to think
If he didn't do something, his home would soon sink
Already the water was deep and rising quite fast
Sam couldn't help but notice a hermit drifting past...

What if he dug a moat around his new home?
Would the water fill it, and leave him alone?
So, he dug and he dug, with his giant crab claw
Stopping suddenly at what he suddenly saw

For what he saw coming, made him quite sad
(Especially after working as hard as he had)
The water still oozed over the top of his trench
And trickled right up to the foot of his bench

Sam's home toppled over and drifted away
And, to his dismay…
He was floating alone, on top of the bay

8

On top of the bay, Sam drifted and cried
And worried about the next coming tide

By this time he was tired and fell fast asleep
Dreaming of the water that surely would creep
Right up to his house he'd been trying to save
From the mouth of the sea, and the Great Tidal Wave

Drifting and dreaming, Sam dropped with a thud
He was wading in murk, dripping with mud
By now, Samuel was stark raving mad!
He was no longer crying, no longer sad!

He decided that moment, right then and right there
To build a great dam for the water to snare
So, he set out to work, there was work to get done
He had to be finished by quarter-to-one
When the tides came back, he'd be ready at least
Yes, Sam was a fighter and the Sea was his beast!

The first thing he did was collect more sticks
He stacked them,
And tied them,
And patched them real quick

Then he set out to find some very big stones
He carried them each to the throne of his home
He HEAVED and he HOED, and he dragged them along
Complaining no more, he was singing a song

10

He worked very hard and built up quite a sweat
From searching the shore, every rock he could get
In the end, he made two-hundred-and-thirty-two trips
While carrying his load on his back and his hips
For the sake of his home he was trying to save
Before it was ruined by the Great Tidal Wave!

One rock at a time, he stacked those great big rocks
While seagulls soared above mocking in flocks
One rock at a time, he formed a great wall
When he was finished, it scaled **10 feet tall**

Just as Sam stopped and admired the art of his work
The gulls began shouting, the Hermits went berserk!

They all pointed to the sea and the monstrous wave
That threatened the hut Sam was trying to save
Sam had been so proud of his newly built dam
He didn't notice until the CRASH! And, the BAM!
The wave inched closer; it was talking
Was it saying "SAAAAAAAAAAAAM?"

The clouds grew dark and loud thunder clapped
If the water got over, they'd all be trapped
The wave rose and licked the top of the rocks
The smart seagulls soared higher in their flocks

But then, just then
The noise went away
The wave, defeated,
Oozed back out to the bay
YEAHHHHHHHHH!

Sam couldn't believe what his eyes were seeing
The waves were leaving, possibly fleeing!

He did it! He did it! Sam saved his new home
Finally, a place that he could call his own!
So, Sam leaned back, and yawned a big yawn
And fiddled a tune that night until dawn

From his porch on the sand of the shore

Of the sandy, white beach, called Corte Magore

16

None have told this tale before…

THE END